Thornton W. Burgess
Nature Stories
TO READ ALOUD

Illustrated by ADRIANNA MAZZA

WONDER BOOKS • NEW YORK

Note to Parents

One of the most gratifying ways of bringing the precious feeling of closeness to your family is sharing the joys of reading with your children. More and more parents are discovering the pleasures of a daily Storytime Hour . . . a time for reading aloud to young children, helping them develop a lifetime love of books, stimulating their imagination, enriching their vocabularies, and teaching them fascinating facts about the world around them.

Read-Aloud books are especially planned for the small child who loves to listen to a story—and also for the beginning reader who is proud of his new talent and wants to show it off for your approval.

You will enjoy reading these stories to your young children. You will enjoy them perhaps even more when your child proudly reads the stories to you.

CONTENTS

THE GROUCHY ONE

There is no gain in being cross,
The end is almost always loss.
                    —Old Mother Nature.

BOBBY COON and Mrs. Coon had only three in the family this year. It was the smallest family they had had for some time. Mother Coon was a little relieved because it meant less work. The more children, the more worries a mother has. Three could provide plenty of worries and did. Now one of these was called Grouchy. You know, one who is selfish, cranky and always finding fault is called a grouch. This young Coon had been that way ever since he was born. He didn't get along with his brothers and sisters. He didn't get along with his mother. He was forever being scolded for doing things he shouldn't do. At the same time, he was one of those smarties who think they know everything there is to know. He was with Brother and Sister and Mother when they met Jimmy Skunk coming along the Crooked Little Path.

Now Mother Coon was most polite to Jimmy Skunk, although she was very much bigger than Jimmy. She stepped out of the Crooked Little Path to let him pass. She not only stepped out of the path, but she stepped to quite a little distance. The three young Coons just didn't know what to make of her. It was the first time they had ever seen Mother Coon step aside for anybody, even for their father, Bobby Coon. After Jimmy Skunk had passed on and was out of sight, the three young Coons crowded around Mother. They wanted to know who that was.

"That," said Mother, "was Jimmy Skunk. Whenever you meet Jimmy Skunk, be polite to him."

"Why?" asked Grouchy.

"Because if you don't, you'll be sorry," replied Mother.

"Will he be very sorry?" asked one of the others.

"Yes," replied his mother. "He'll be very, very sorry."

"I don't see why," said the other. "He doesn't look dangerous. He isn't as big as you and he doesn't look as strong as you."

"You can't always tell by looks," replied Mother Coon. "Jimmy Skunk doesn't fight."

"Then why is there any need of being polite to him unless one wants to be polite?" Grouchy asked.

"Because," replied Mother Coon, "he has always with him a little bag of scent. And when he throws a little of that scent, you just have to get away and get away quick."

"Do you mean really run away?" asked one of the others.

"I sure do. And how!" explained Mother.

Later, when the three young Coons were off by themselves, Grouchy declared that he wasn't afraid of that Jimmy Skunk. He laughed at the idea of being afraid of scent and running away from it. "Some day I'll show him he can't scare me," he boasted.

"WHO ARE YOU?"

Through impoliteness much is lost,
And often at too great a cost.
                        —Old Mother Nature.

GROUCHY, one of Bobby Coon's three half-grown children, had a bad disposition. That is why he was called Grouchy. His brother and sister didn't like to play with him. No one liked to have him around. Grouchy people have few friends.

Now Grouchy had taken to going off by himself to get acquainted with the Great World. He never went a great ways from the others, but he seemed to like his own company best and was always lagging behind or going to one side or the other or running ahead. This evening he had run ahead and who should he come face to face with but Jimmy Skunk. Jimmy was ambling along the Crooked Little Path, minding his own business as he always does. That is the way with independent people, and Jimmy is the most independent of all the Green Forest and Green Meadows folk.

It had happened a few nights before that Grouchy had seen his mother step aside for Jimmy Skunk. Afterward he had boasted to his brother and sister that if ever he should meet Jimmy Skunk he wouldn't step aside. Now he was face to face with Jimmy. Should he or should he not step aside? Of course, the polite thing to do would be to give Jimmy the right of way.

But Grouchy cared nothing about politeness. He never was polite unless he was forced to be. Grouchy folks are like that. Grouchiness is nearly always impolite. One never hears of a polite grouchy person. So now the young Coon stopped still in the middle of the path.

"Hello, young fellow," said Jimmy Skunk. "You must be one of Mother Coon's children that I saw the other night."

"What of it?" growled Grouchy.

"Nothing," replied Jimmy Skunk. "I guess Mother has forgotten to teach you politeness. I suggest that you step aside for me to pass."

"Who are you to tell me what I should and should not do?" demanded the young Coon most impolitely.

"I'm just a friend trying to keep you out of trouble," replied Jimmy Skunk. And that is just what he was doing. Jimmy is not at all quick-tempered and he was keeping his temper now. He moved a step or two ahead, expecting the young Coon to back up. Instead, Grouchy growled. "I'm not afraid of you," growled Grouchy. "You needn't think you can order me around."

Jimmy stopped and looked very hard at the young Coon. Should he or should he not teach this young Coon a lesson? He certainly deserved one.

Just then, Mother and the other two young Coons appeared, shuffling along the Crooked Little Path. When Mother saw Grouchy and Jimmy Skunk up ahead she hurried forward. She didn't like at all what she saw. Jimmy was standing with his big plume of a tail straight up in the air. It was a danger signal. She knew that, but Grouchy didn't.

MOTHER INTERFERES

Be always sure that it is clear,
You know just when to interfere.
— Old Mother Nature.

WHAT Old Mother Nature says is very important. To interfere at just the right time is very good. To interfere at the wrong time can be just as bad. In most quarrels too many people make the mistake of interfering at the wrong time.

Mother Coon was startled. In fact, Mother Coon was quite upset. She had come along just in time to see one of her children, the bad-tempered one called Grouchy, growling at Jimmy Skunk and refusing to get out of Jimmy's way. Jimmy's big spreading banner of a tail was standing straight up. Mother knew only too well what that meant. It was a danger signal. It was a warning. She looked hastily at the tip of that tail. It still drooped

11

down. If that tail should suddenly move farther over his back it would be just too bad for everybody in the neighborhood except Jimmy himself. And it would be especially too bad for foolish young Grouchy.

Jimmy Skunk knew that Mother Coon knew how foolish it would be to interfere with him. He could afford to be a little patient and he was. He would give Mother Coon a chance to get that foolish youngster out of the way. So, all he did was to stamp his feet as an extra warning to keep out of trouble.

"What is he doing that for?" asked one of the other young Coons, who was looking on.

"It is a warning you always want to heed when you hear it," replied his mother. "When Jimmy Skunk stamps, make very sure that you are not too near."

"I don't see why," growled Grouchy, who was still holding the path.

"You will if you don't watch out," replied his mother, as she came alongside him. Then she gave him a push right out of the Crooked Little Path. She followed it up by boxing his ears. He ran to get away from her. Mother followed him for a little ways. Jimmy Skunk lowered his tail. He no longer stamped. He

12

ambled along on his way as if nothing had happened.

That was just like Jimmy Skunk. He doesn't seem to pick a quarrel. He doesn't run away from others who seek to interfere with him. And in the end he usually walks off just as he was doing now. And he doesn't think any more about what has happened. He understood perfectly that that young Coon was a smarty. He deserved to be punished and Mother was boxing his ears and that was enough. Jimmy is the most independent of all the folk who use the Crooked Little Path through the Green Forest or the Lone Little Path across the Green Meadows. Wherever he goes he is treated with respect, mostly because folks have learned it doesn't pay not to. Jimmy always stands up for his rights. But also, he respects the rights of others. That is another reason why he is so independent.

Meanwhile Grouchy was running away from Mother. She hoped he had learned his lesson, but she doubted it very much. Grouchy didn't appear in the least bit sorry for what he had done. He hadn't yet really learned that impoliteness doesn't pay.

GROUCHY SHOWS OFF

Showing off will seldom pay,
Friends are quickly lost that way.
                              —Jimmy Skunk.

GROUCHY, the young Coon who had been impolite to Jimmy Skunk and whose ears Mother Coon had boxed because of it, still hadn't learned his lesson. He had a good opinion of himself. It is never well to have too good an opinion of one's self. It almost always leads to trouble. Grouchy was still sure that he could make Jimmy Skunk step aside for him and he hoped to have a chance to show his brother and sister that he wasn't afraid to do it.

The chance came over in the Old Pasture. They were all over there one evening when who should come down one of the old cow paths but Jimmy Skunk. Jolly, round, bright

Mistress Moon was shining her brightest. It was almost as light over there as by day.

"Here comes your friend," said his sister to Grouchy.

"Let's see you make him get out of your way," said his mischievous brother.

Grouchy swelled all up with good opinion of himself. He strutted. Yes, sir, he strutted. People who like to show off always strut. It is one of the easiest ways of showing off. It looks as if it meant a great deal and it doesn't mean a thing, excepting how foolish the strutter is. He walked right out into that path in front of Jimmy Skunk.

Jimmy Skunk stopped. "So, it is you again," said he, mildly.

"Yes, it is me. And this time Mother isn't around to interfere," declared Grouchy.

"That's too bad," said Jimmy. Then he added, "For you."

"Not for me, but for you," retorted the young Coon impudently.

"I don't like young folks to do silly things," said Jimmy Skunk.

"Who's doing foolish things?" growled Grouchy.

"A certain young Coon who should know

better, after what his mother has told him," replied Jimmy Skunk.

"I'm not afraid of you," retorted the young Coon. He was boasting.

"That's just too bad, because you ought to be afraid of me," replied Jimmy Skunk. "That is, you ought to be afraid to interfere with me. No one needs to be afraid of me who doesn't interfere. I don't go about looking for trouble. But when trouble comes my way it usually goes away again with the other fellow, not with me."

"Pooh!" exclaimed the young Coon, and showed all his teeth.

"Don't do that. I don't like it," said Jimmy Skunk.

"If you feel them, you will like it still less," boasted Grouchy.

Slowly Jimmy Skunk's big tail began to rise. "I'm giving you fair warning," said he.

"I don't care anything about your old warning. A warning never hurt anybody. And I don't think you can either," boasted the young Coon, and looked around at his brother and sister for admiration.

As a matter of fact, his brother and sister looked more scared than admiring.

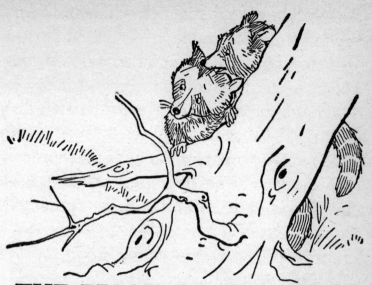

THE PRICE OF BOASTING

No matter what, both bad or nice,
For everything you pay a price.

　　　　　　　　　—Jimmy Skunk.

A FOOLISH young boaster over in the Old Pasture was getting ready for trouble, but he didn't know it. He was duly warned, but he didn't heed the warning. He was being impudent to Jimmy Skunk and that is the last person in the world that anyone should be impudent to. Now, Jimmy is not quick-tempered. Far from it. It is only once in a while that Jimmy loses his temper, but that is only when he is attacked or provoked.

But Jimmy is independent and he doesn't allow any interference with his independence. He had been coming down an old cow path over in the Old Pasture and had met young Grouchy, the half-grown son of Bobby Coon. His brother and sister were with Grouchy. They promptly stopped when they saw Jimmy Skunk coming, but Grouchy didn't. He didn't stop until they met almost face to face.

Jimmy expected the young Coon to step aside and leave the path clear for him. He was in the habit of having everybody he met do that. But young Grouchy did nothing of the kind. He foolishly ordered Jimmy Skunk to get out of his way. He was showing off before his brother and sister.

It happened that none of the young Coons knew anything about Jimmy Skunk. Only once before had they met him and Mother was with them then. Mother had shown him the greatest politeness. They couldn't understand it. Jimmy didn't look like a fighter. He didn't look dangerous at all. Yet Mother had treated him with the greatest respect. What could it mean?

Now Jimmy Skunk was beginning to lose

patience. He ordered Grouchy to get out of
the path. He warned him he would be sorry if
he didn't. His big plumy tail was standing
straight up. That was a warning. The trouble
was that Grouchy didn't know just what that
warning meant. He didn't know what would
happen if he failed to heed that warning. The
young Coon was impudent, very impudent.

Jimmy had told him that he was giving him fair warning.

"I don't care anything about your old warning. A warning never yet hurt anybody and I don't believe you can either," declared Grouchy in the sauciest manner. He looked over his shoulder to see if his brother and sister were admiring his boldness. They were not. They were two scared-looking young Coons, although they didn't yet know what they were scared of.

Jimmy Skunk suddenly stamped with his front feet. When Jimmy stamps that way it means that he is losing patience. It is another warning. When Jimmy stamps that way, anyone very near him will, if he is wise, move away. Jimmy is very fair-minded. He gives everybody a chance. He doesn't take folks by surprise as some others do.

The young Coon showed all his teeth and growled. The hair on his neck and shoulders stood on end, making him look more fierce than he really was. He took a step toward Jimmy Skunk. Then it was that something happened, a dreadful thing. Young Grouchy learned a lesson and for it paid the price of boasting. And it was a rather dreadful price.

THE LESSON

In bitterness are some things learned,
And painfully is knowledge earned.
                —Old Mother Nature.

THERE was a bad smell over in the Old Pasture. Anyway, most folks thought it was a bad smell. There was just one person responsible for that bad smell in the Old Pasture and that was Grouchy, half-grown son of Bobby and Mrs. Coon. It wouldn't have happened had Mother been along. Perhaps it was just as well she wasn't along, because now Grouchy had learned a lesson. Anyway, he was learning a lesson. He had been impudent to Jimmy Skunk. And Jimmy had taught him that it doesn't pay to be impolite.

Grouchy didn't yet know what had happened. Jimmy had stamped his feet as a warning. Grouchy hadn't heeded that warning. Then something had happened that Grouchy couldn't understand at all. His eyes had been filled with something that blinded them. It made them smart and he couldn't see at all. His nose had been filled with a dreadful odor, the worst smell he had ever known, and it was so strong it choked him. He hadn't supposed there was anywhere in all the Great World such a smell. He rolled over and over on the ground, but he couldn't roll away from it. He got to his feet and tried to run, but he couldn't yet see very well. His eyes still smarted. And worst of all, he carried that smell along with him.

Grouchy had been showing off before his brother and sister. They had not taken any part in the impoliteness to Jimmy Skunk. They had simply looked on from a safe distance. Now, of course, they got the dreadful smell, but not as much as their foolish young brother. They both turned and ran and they soon ran away from it. That was something that Grouchy couldn't do. You see, none of the scent that Jimmy had thrown had touched

the other two young Coons. But it had all gone
into the fur of Grouchy. So, of course he
couldn't run away from it. He had to carry
it away with him wherever he went.

Jimmy Skunk paid no attention to what
Grouchy might do. He lowered his tail and
ambled on down the little cow path quite as

if nothing at all had happened. Meanwhile, Grouchy was choking and trying to get his breath. At the same time, he was stopping every few steps to rub his eyes with his paws and even now he didn't know what had happened to him. He did know, however, that never again would he go too near a Skunk. He didn't think that Jimmy Skunk used a fair way of fighting. You see, he didn't stop to think that it was all his own fault. Had he been polite and stepped aside for Jimmy Skunk, as a young person always should step aside for an older person, it wouldn't have happened.

Young Grouchy suddenly met Reddy Fox. Now, at any other time Reddy would have been ready to pounce on him. But Reddy did nothing of the kind now. He wrinkled up his nose and made a bad face. Then he grinned and stepped aside.

"How did you enjoy meeting Jimmy Skunk?" asked Reddy.

Grouchy said nothing. He simply tried to run away, for he was frightened worse than ever. He didn't yet realize that because of that dreadful smell he was in no danger whatever from Reddy Fox.

GROUCHY'S LOST APPETITE

Sickness, worry, sudden fright,
Cause the loss of appetite.
          —Old Mother Nature.

YOUNG GROUCHY, half-grown son of Bobby Coon, had lost his appetite. Yes, sir, he had lost his appetite. He just couldn't eat. He couldn't bear to think of eating. That was a bad state for a half-grown young Coon to be in. He had started out early that evening with a big appetite, the kind of an appetite a growing young Coon should have. Then he had met Jimmy Skunk and Jimmy had taken away his appetite.

Anyway, that is the way Grouchy thought

about it. He had had the appetite until he met Jimmy Skunk and since then had had no appetite at all. That was because he was being taught a lesson. He had been impolite to Jimmy Skunk and now he was learning that impoliteness never pays. Jimmy Skunk had thrown, full in his face, the bad scent which he carries with him to protect himself from enemies. That scent had gone all into his coat and he couldn't get rid of it. No matter where he went, he took the bad smell with him. He tried rolling in the mud at the edge of Laughing Brook, but he still had that dreadful smell and no appetite. Once he surprised a young Frog almost under his nose. He was very fond of young Frogs. But he allowed this one to hop right out from between his paws. He didn't want a young Frog to eat. He didn't want to eat anything.

Mother and his brother and sister had gone up to Farmer Brown's field for corn in the milk, than which there is nothing Raccoons like quite so well. Grouchy didn't want corn in the milk. He didn't want any corn at all. There was only one thing in the world that that young Coon wanted. And he wanted that as he never wanted anything before. It was to get rid of that dreadful smell. If he could just do that, he wouldn't care what happened.

Once he met Jumper the Hare over in the Green Forest. Jumper hastened to circle around so that the wind blew from him to the young Coon instead of the other way. He grinned at young Grouchy.

"How is Jimmy Skunk this evening?" he inquired.

"I don't know anything about Jimmy Skunk. He is no friend of mine," retorted the young Coon.

Jumper chuckled. "I think he is a very good friend of yours," said he.

"What do you mean?" demanded Grouchy.

"I think he has fixed it so that nobody in the world will touch you. And if that isn't being a true friend, what is?" replied Jumper. "By the way," he added, "I hear that the first grapes are beginning to ripen."

"I don't want any grapes," growled the young Coon.

"Oh!" exclaimed Jumper. "I thought all Coons were fond of grapes."

"I've lost my appetite," growled Grouchy.

"I thought you might have," chuckled Jumper, hopping away.

THE FAMILY OUTCAST

Some things e'en love will not condone,
And must be suffered quite alone.
—Mother Coon.

WHAT Mother Coon says is true. Young
Grouchy, one of her three half-grown
children, was finding it out. Something had
happened to him that he never dreamed could
happen to him. He was an outcast. That
means that he was no longer welcome in his
own home. Not only did he lack a welcome
there, but he was actually driven away. His

brother and sister and his mother wouldn't allow him in the house nor anywhere near it if they were about. He had to go live by himself.

It was fully his own fault. Yes, sir, there was nobody to blame but himself. He did blame someone else, but he had no right to. It was Jimmy Skunk. He felt that Jimmy was the cause of all his misery at the present time. But the real cause was his own impudence to Jimmy Skunk. He had refused to get out of Jimmy's way when Jimmy had warned him that he would be sorry if he didn't. He was sorry. What is more, he was going to be sorry for a long time. But he didn't know this. You see, Jimmy Skunk had used his little bag of scent. Jimmy and the members of his family may like that special scent, but no one else does. Most folks think it is rather dreadful. Young Grouchy did. He had even lost his appetite, and anything that can take away a growing Coon's appetite must be bad indeed.

Mother had not been with the three young Coons when they had met Jimmy Skunk and Grouchy had been impolite. As a matter of fact, she had been at home in a certain big hollow tree. Grouchy had gone straight there

after his trouble with Jimmy Skunk. Mother
Coon had heard him whimpering and whining
as he approached the foot of the tree. She
had put her head out the doorway. Then she
had wrinkled her nose and made a face. She
had caught that dreadful smell. "Go away!"
she barked. "You can't come in here!"

"But I want to," whined the young Coon. "I don't feel well."

"You don't smell well either," retorted his mother. "You've been impolite to Jimmy Skunk and now it serves you right. There's no place for you here."

"But what can I do?" whined Grouchy.

"You can live by yourself and you'll have to," retorted his mother.

"But I don't want to live alone," he whined.

"What you want to do has nothing to do with the matter. It is what you've got to do. Had you heeded the warning I gave you, this wouldn't have happened. But it has happened and now you can make the best of it by yourself." Mother's voice was harsh.

Grouchy remembered a certain hollow log not very far from there and went over to it. He crawled inside and there he sulked until a little later he heard his brother and sister outside. By this time he was feeling better. He crawled out of the old log to join them. The two young Coons sniffed once or twice, then turned and took to their heels. They didn't want to have anything to do with their bad-smelling brother. Young Grouchy was still learning the lesson he had been given.

A LESSON REALLY LEARNED

A lesson learned has small excuse,
Until it has been put to use.
—Old Mother Nature.

SOME lessons are short and quickly learned. Sometimes lessons of that kind are soon forgotten. Other lessons are long and hard. Lessons of this kind usually are better remembered, sometimes never forgotten. It was a lesson of this kind that Grouchy, half-grown son of Bobby and Mrs. Coon, had learned.

Grouchy had always been headstrong, wanting his own way, thinking himself a little smarter than others. Then he had met Jimmy Skunk and Jimmy had taught him the lesson that Mother Coon had tried in vain to teach him.

Mother had warned never to be impolite to Jimmy Skunk and always treat him with respect. Then one day, when Mother was not with them, Grouchy and his brother and sister met Jimmy Skunk up in the Old Pasture. Grouchy tried to show off. He ordered Jimmy Skunk out of his way. He refused to heed the warning Jimmy Skunk gave him. So Jimmy gave him something more than a warning. He sprayed the young Coon with the scent that is famous for being bad-smelling. That was bad enough at the time. It got in Grouchy's eyes and blinded him for a while. It got up his nose and made him choke and strangle. He thought at the time nothing could be worse. But that was only the beginning of the lesson he was to learn. He lost his appetite right then and there and it was several days before he really got it back. But worst of all was the fact that he carried that dreadful smell with him. It was in his coat and he couldn't get rid of it. Of course he couldn't take his coat off and leave it behind. Sometimes he wished he could.

No one would have anything to do with him. A very dreadful thing happened when he went whining and crying home. Mother wouldn't let him in the house. Brother and sister wouldn't play with him. He had to find another place in which to sleep. He did. It was an old log that was hollow. He crept into

that and there he was safe. He was safe because that dreadful smell hung around the old log because it was in his coat. On account of that smell no one would come near the old log.

But he soon found out that none of the neighbors would have anything to do with him. For a while that made him more bad-tempered than ever. But after a while he got used to it. Then, because he could no longer travel with Mother and his brother and sister, he had to learn to do everything for himself. So he learned faster than the others did. As soon as he got back his appetite he began to grow faster and he soon was quite equal to taking care of himself under all circumstances. Living alone now wasn't so bad. He felt quite equal to holding his own. But the lesson he had learned he had really learned. Whenever he met Jimmy Skunk he took pains to be perfectly polite. If they met on the Crooked Little Path or the Lone Little Path or any other path, Grouchy always stepped out of the path and politely walked around Jimmy Skunk. The result was that, in a manner of speaking, they became friends. Things do work out that way sometimes.

WHY IT PAYS TO BE POLITE

You will find in countless ways,
How politeness really pays.
                    —Old Mother Nature.

MOTHER COON with two half-grown children were headed for Farmer Brown's cornfield where the corn was in the milk. Grouchy, the third of the three children that made up Mrs. Coon's little family, was not with them. He wanted to be, but they wouldn't have him. Mother wouldn't allow him anywhere near. That was because wherever he went he carried with him the dreadful smell with which Jimmy Skunk had filled his coat. This would have been bad enough had it lasted only for a little while. But it lasted for a long while. In fact, it seemed as if Grouchy was never going to get rid of it.

It happened that Grouchy's brother and sister had seen what had happened to him. In fact, he had been showing off for their benefit when he refused to step out of Jimmy Skunk's way. He had told Jimmy Skunk that he wasn't afraid of him. And he really hadn't been at the time. This was because he knew almost nothing about Jimmy Skunk. He was warned by his mother, but had to have a painful lesson before he would believe what he had been told. He had to find out by experience. And he had found out. Experience is a rough teacher sometimes, but a teacher who makes one learn.

Now, after seeing what had happened to their brother, the two others were very much afraid of Jimmy Skunk. And when they met Jimmy Skunk over in Farmer Brown's cornfield they were for leaving at once or going to another part of the field. They were afraid to go near Jimmy.

But it wasn't so with Mother. She most politely passed the time of day with Jimmy. She was polite and he was polite.

"I judge you like corn as well as we Coons do," said Mother

"Right, Mrs. Coon. Quite right. We Skunks

are very fond of it when it is at this stage, just nice and milky. I only have to make one or two trips over here while the corn is at its best," said Jimmy.

Mother Coon walked up almost beside Jimmy Skunk. She didn't seem in the least afraid of him. She wasn't. She and Jimmy understood each other. Where there is understanding of one another there is seldom trouble. She knew as long as she didn't interfere with Jimmy Skunk he wouldn't interfere with her. And as long as she was polite to him he would be polite to her.

Watching from some distance away, for they were still afraid, the two young Coons didn't know just what to make of it. They had seen what had happened to their brother, but now nothing of the kind happened to Mother. Mother went about pulling down stalks of corn and tearing open the ears to take just a bite or two from each. She was being terribly wasteful, but she didn't care.

Little by little the two young Coons began to understand that this was one way in which politeness pays. If they were polite to Jimmy Skunk, they would have nothing to be afraid of from him.

WHAT GROUCHY FOUND OUT

With some things learned nothing's lost,
No matter what may be the cost.
  —Old Mother Nature.

HOW TRUE that saying is! Grouchy, the unhappy young Coon who had been in trouble with Jimmy Skunk, was finding out. The lesson he had learned, the cost of impoliteness, had been a hard one. It hadn't been short as some lessons are. It had lasted a long time and all the time he had had to keep much by himself. Nobody wanted him around. That was because he carried the bad scent of Jimmy Skunk with him. It was in his coat and he couldn't get it out.

Because Mother and Father and his brother and sister would have almost nothing to do with him, he had to spend most of his time by himself. And he had to learn many things by doing them. There is no better way of learning than by doing. The trouble with too many folks is that they have too much done for them. Grouchy didn't have anything done for him now. He had to find all his own food. At first he did this by following at a distance behind the rest of the family and eating what they had left. But after a while he found that he could live much better if he was completely independent, if he first found and got the food for himself. He slept through the day and each night started out for himself—and each night he felt a little more independent.

On the other hand, his brother and sister, who had Mother with them all the time, were not learning nearly so fast how to take care of themselves. Mother was always somewhere near to warn them of possible danger. Mother called them to share in things she had found that were especially good. Grouchy had to find such things for himself. Thus it was that he found out what it meant to be independent and that there was nothing else quite like it. There came a time when he wouldn't have gone back to live with the others if he had been asked. He was out in the Great World for himself. And he was proud of it.

These nights when he met Jimmy Skunk he kept at a safe distance. At first he was resentful. He growled and snarled at Jimmy from a safe distance. Jimmy never paid any attention to him. Jimmy went about his own business just as if there was no one else near. After a while Grouchy stopped growling and snarling. He became respectful. He found that if he was polite, Jimmy was polite and that each could go about his own business.

In time, that dreadful odor from Jimmy Skunk's bag of scent disappeared. The time came when it could be smelled in his coat only when his coat was damp. Then there came a time when there was none of that dreadful odor at all. He could go where he pleased insofar as other folks were concerned. No one tried to drive him away. He could join his mother and father and brother and sister if he wanted to. But strangely enough, he didn't want to. He preferred to be alone. And that is what came from the lesson he was taught by Jimmy Skunk. It cost him a lot of unhappiness, but independence was worth all it had cost.

BUSTER BEAR
DOESN'T KNOW

Happy-go-lucky folk never will plan,
They take things each day the best they can.
                        —Old Mother Nature.

BUSTER BEAR is one of the happy-go-lucky-folk. Nowhere in all the Green Forest is there anyone quite so happy-go-lucky. He never worries about what may happen next. He takes things as they come, good or bad, and makes the best of them.

"G-r-r-r-r-r!" growled Buster.

Chatterer the Red Squirrel jumped almost out of his skin. He had just pulled a fat sweet acorn out of one of his storerooms in an old stump. Of course he dropped the acorn. He made a wild jump to a neighboring tree and from a short distance up he began to scold, and how! When he had gone down to that stump to get that acorn he hadn't known that Buster Bear was anywhere near. Buster had been having a nap under some low boughs, and because he hadn't moved when Chatterer first came, the latter hadn't seen him.

The dropped acorn rolled almost to Buster's nose. He reached out a big paw and pulled it in. He ate it and smacked his lips. Then he licked them. Buster dearly loved fat acorns. "G-r-r-r-r!" growled Buster again, and got to his feet. Chatterer continued to scold. Then he became furious.

"I thought you had gone to bed for the winter," he said. "When are you going?"

"I don't know," growled Buster.

"When you do go, where will you go to bed?" demanded Chatterer.

"I don't know," growled Buster.

"Do you think it is going to be a hard winter?" Chatterer asked next.

"I don't know," growled Buster.

"If you stay awake much longer, where will

you get food enough?" demanded Chatterer.

"I don't know," growled Buster.

"Where is Mrs. Bear these days?" the red-coated scamp in the tree asked.

"I don't know," growled Buster.

"Do you think she's gone to sleep yet?" Chatterer persisted.

"I don't know," growled Buster.

Chatterer was losing patience. "You don't know much, do you?" he squeaked.

"I don't know," growled Buster.

Chatterer was quite beside himself. His tongue fairly flew as he scolded again. He even came down the tree head first until he was only a little above Buster's head. As he scolded as fast as his tongue could go, Buster paid no attention to him. He walked over to the old stump from which that acorn had rolled. He put a big paw on it.

"You leave that alone! That's mine!" shrieked Chatterer. And if he had not had to cling to the trunk of the tree with all four feet he probably would have been dancing in rage. "You leave that alone, you big robber!" he cried.

Buster just grinned at him, and Chatterer didn't like the looks of those big teeth.

WHOSE ACORNS
WERE THEY?

Be things in big or small amounts,
Possession is the thing that counts.
                    —Buster Bear.

BUSTER BEAR looked up at Chatterer the Red Squirrel and grinned. Then he dug his big claws into the old stump from which an acorn had rolled. Chatterer had been sitting on that stump and had dropped that acorn when Buster Bear had first appeared.

Buster pulled. The big claws dug into the bark and pulled off a big piece. The wood under that bark was not very strong. You see, that was an old stump, and the minute

Buster put his paw on it he knew it was hollow. Buster dug his claws in a little deeper and pulled a little harder. Chatterer screamed at the top of his voice, calling Buster Bear a robber, thief and other bad things. With every bad name he jerked his red tail until it seemed as if he might jerk that tail right off. He always jerks his tail when he scolds.

"G-r-r-r-r-r!" growled Buster and gave a hard pull. Out fell a piece of that old stump and out after it fell a lot of big, plump, sweet acorns. Chatterer screamed as if he would scream his head off. You see, that old stump was one of his storerooms. He had put all those fat sweet acorns in there to have through the winter. Buster looked over at Chatterer and grinned once more. Then he began picking up those sweet acorns and chewing them up as fast as he could. "M-m-m-m-m-m! These are good!" said Buster.

"They're mine, you big thief!" shrieked the red-coated little Squirrel. "They're mine!"

"You don't say," said Buster. "If they're yours, why don't you come and get them? They are the best acorns I've had for a long,

long time. I didn't know you were putting
away any for me."

"I didn't put them away for you!" shrieked
Chatterer.

"It seems so to me," said Buster, and picked
up some more.

When Buster had picked up all the acorns that had rolled out he once more turned to the old stump. He hooked the claws of his big front paws into the sides of the old stump and tore it apart. There were a lot more acorns still in there. And there were a lot of little three-sided beechnuts. Acorns are good, but beechnuts are still better to Buster Bear and he was having a feast. The truth is, Buster had had very little to eat for several days. He should have been abed and asleep, because that is what he does when his food supply fails. In fact, he was thinking of going about it when he had discovered Chatterer and the acorn. Now he could stay awake a little longer. Perhaps if he looked about he could find another of Chatterer's storehouses. He well knew that this wasn't the only one.

When the last little nut had disappeared Buster looked over at Chatterer. "How about showing me another storehouse?" he asked. Then he grinned.

Whose acorns and beechnuts were those? Chatterer said they were his because he had found them and stored them away. But Buster just grinned more broadly and said, "I've got 'em now!"

BUSTER BEAR'S BEDTIME

There's a time to work, a time to play,
And a time to sleep in every day.
                              —Old Mother Nature.

IT WAS Buster Bear's bedtime. Anyway, that is what his neighbors in the Green Forest thought. Old Man Winter had arrived. There was little food and that was hard to find. Buster Bear is so big that he needs a lot of food. Usually when he can't get it he goes to sleep. He doesn't need it then. But Buster had not gone to sleep this year. The fact was, he had been unusually lucky in finding food.

Buster is not fussy about his food. He likes just about everything. That is one reason why he can get enough to eat when some other people can't. He eats any kind of meat he can find and he doesn't fuss over it. In fact, Buster is not the least bit fussy. He likes fresh meat, but he doesn't turn up his nose at meat so old that other folks won't touch it. He likes all kinds of fruit. He is fond of nuts. He even likes insects. He sometimes will stir up an ant's nest and lick up the ants as fast as they pour out to see what the trouble is. And how he does love honey and sugar! His love of sweets often gets him into trouble.

His neighbors are not fond of Buster at any time of year because of his big appetite. And so they look forward to the time when he will have such hard work to get enough to eat that he will decide to go to sleep instead.

Buster was shuffling along the Crooked Little Path when he met Reddy Fox. Reddy stopped. So did Buster. "Why haven't you gone to bed for the winter?" demanded Reddy.

"It is not your business," said Buster. "I do as I please. I just don't choose to go to bed yet."

"In other years you've been in bed and asleep by this time. What is keeping you awake? Have you a stomach-ache or something?" Reddy asked, rather impudently.

"The only time my stomach aches is when there's nothing to put in it. That is when I go to sleep and forget things," growled Buster irritably.

"Then that means you are getting things to eat," said Reddy. "I don't know how you do it. I have a hard enough time and I'm not as big as you."

"You're too fussy," grumbled Buster. "Fussy folks deserve to have hard times. I'm not fussy. I eat anything that can be eaten, or pretty near. Yesterday I found a storehouse full of acorns. Chatterer the Red Squirrel said they belonged to him. Perhaps they did once, but when I was through with them they belonged to me and nobody could take them away from me. You don't happen to know where Chatterer has any more stored away, do you?"

"No, I don't. And I wouldn't tell you if I did," declared Reddy. "You'd better go to sleep. If I could do that, I would. I think you're silly."

"How am I silly?" growled Buster.

"You're silly when you can go to sleep and don't do it," retorted Reddy.

"I will when I get ready," growled Buster.

BUSTER HAS THE WANDERING FOOT

Some restless feet are bound to roam,
And never truly have a home.
                    —Old Mother Nature.

THAT IS the kind of feet Buster Bear has. He dearly loves to wander. Some travelers always know just where they're going. The only times that Buster knows exactly where he's going is when he knows exactly where there is something good to eat. Otherwise, he just wanders here and wanders there. So he seldom has to worry about getting anywhere in particular at a particular time. It is a happy-go-lucky way of living. But Buster Bear is a great big happy-go-lucky fellow who has few worries and gets a lot of fun out of living.

Buster should have been asleep. It was

already winter and Buster usually goes to sleep soon after the first snow comes. But this year the snow had been late in coming and even now there wasn't too much of it. So Buster, instead of going to sleep, had taken to wandering. When he feels like wandering Buster can be a great traveler. He travels long distances, miles and miles. That is what he was doing now. He had left the Green Forest at the foot of the Great Mountain and those he had left behind would have been surprised could they have known how far he had gone. This didn't mean that he had gone to stay. He would make a big circle back again.

Reddy Fox was the last one to see him before he left. In the days that followed Reddy missed him. "I do believe that great nuisance took my advice and has gone to sleep," said Reddy to Mrs. Reddy.

"I hope so," replied Mrs. Reddy. "Have you any idea where he may be?"

"Not the least," replied Reddy. "I never have seen such a fellow as Buster Bear. He may be asleep almost anywhere. He may be in a den in the rocks, like Yowler the Bobcat. Or he may be in just a hole in the ground, or he may be under a pile of brush. I don't suppose that fellow himself knows where he is going to bed down until the notion comes to him to do it."

"All I can say is," said Mrs. Reddy, "if Buster has already gone to bed, and I hope he has, I hope also that he'll stay asleep all winter. Food is bound to be hard enough to find for us Foxes without having to share it with that fellow."

Meanwhile, Buster's wandering feet were taking him into all sorts of places—up in the mountains, out in the pastures on the edges of farms, along brooks, the shores of ponds and lakes. Up hill and down dale wandered Buster and somehow he managed to find enough food to keep him going. Once he broke into a lonely camp where some supplies had been left. He had a full stomach when he left. Finally he turned and began to go back toward where he had started. He was really getting ready for his winter's sleep without knowing it. Each day food was a little harder to find. And each day the urge to get back was a little greater. His wandering feet were taking him home, if he could be said to have a home.

BUSTER IS TOO LATE

For some it seems to be their fate,
To always be a bit too late.

> —Old Mother Nature.

BUSTER BEAR was back in the Green Forest at the foot of the Great Mountain. His wandering feet had taken him many, many miles away and back again. There was no one to welcome him back, because the neighbors there would have been just as pleased and a little more so if he hadn't come back at all. You see, it was winter and times were hard. At such a time the more people there are the less food there is to go around.

Now Buster Bear's plan of life is very simple. It is to eat as long as there is anything to eat and then sleep until once more there is something to eat. One reason he had wandered so far was that in that way he could keep awake longer because he could find more food. But now he was back. There was nothing to eat and he began to think about going to sleep. There was a certain big brush pile. At some time in a great storm a number of trees had fallen over in a great pile. Such a pile of fallen trees is called a windfall. Buster knew all about that windfall. He had been under it for a nap more than once. He decided that that was just the place to go to sleep for the remainder of the winter. He shuffled over to it. Buster's walk is apt to be a shuffle, but it takes him along fast. He reached the big windfall. Just outside of it sat Jumper the Hare. Buster couldn't catch Jumper if he tried, so he didn't try. He is smart that way. He doesn't try to do things he can't do. From a safe distance Jumper spoke. "I thought you'd gone away, Buster Bear," he declared.

"I've come back," said Buster.

"What for?" Jumper wanted to know.

"To go to bed," replied Buster. "I think it's time I went to sleep for the winter."

"The rest of us have thought so for some time," said Jumper. "Where are you going to sleep?"

"Right under this great pile," said Buster.

"No, you're not," declared Jumper.

"Who says I'm not?" growled Buster.

"I do," said Jumper.

Buster looked puzzled. He was puzzled. What could Jumper the Hare know about things that were only his own concern? "How do you know what I'm going to or not going to do?" growled Buster.

"I know you're not going to bed under there for the winter," said Jumper. "Someone else is under there already."

Buster suddenly sat up very straight and stared at the pile of brush. "Who is under there?" he demanded.

"Mrs. Bear," replied Jumper. "She went to bed there some time ago. Are you going to wake her up?"

"Not if I know it," replied Buster.

BUSTER TURNS BURGLAR

*Some folks still seem to think that might
Alone decided just what is right.*
>   —Old Mother Nature.

THAT IS true. There are still some folks who think that might makes right. Of course it does nothing of the kind. Instead of that it often makes two wrongs out of one. A thing is wrong or it is right, regardless of what you want it to be.

Buster Bear was a disappointed Bear. He had finally made up his mind to go to sleep for the rest of the winter and he had headed for a great pile of brush, called a windfall, deep in the Green Forest. Underneath that he had often taken a nap through the summer. He decided it would be just the place to spend the rest of the winter. When he got there he was forced to change his mind. Mrs. Bear was already in there under that brush asleep. Not for the world would Buster waken her.

So he turned his back on the old windfall and went wandering about, uncertain just where to go to sleep for the rest of the winter. At the moment he was feeling more cross than sleepy. Growling to himself, he wandered here and there and finally found himself among the maple trees where, every year in the spring, Farmer Brown made maple syrup and maple sugar. There in front of Buster was the sugarhouse. Buster stood still and stared at it. It was deserted. Farmer Brown and Farmer Brown's Boy were nowhere around. What was more, they hadn't been around for a long time. Buster knew this because he could find no man scent at all.

Buster sniffed all around the little house. There was no man smell, but there was still some sugar smell and it made his mouth water. He drooled. Yes, sir, he drooled. That sweet smell made him drool. He climbed up on the roof. He climbed down again. Nowhere could he find an opening. Finally he did discover a crack into which he could get the claws of a forefoot. He dug his claws in. He pulled. He puffed. He pulled and tugged harder still. A big splinter pulled out. It was easier to get his claws in now and get hold. Presently he had torn a hole that he could put a big paw through. Now it was easier to tug and pull.

Buster forgot he was sleepy. He forgot all about the windfall and Mrs. Buster. He had no thought for anything but the mischief he was now in. To him it wasn't mischief. He meant to get into the little house—and the harder it was to do it, the more determined he became. At long last he broke his way in. He sniffed and he sniffed and he sniffed, and every sniff made his mouth water, but look as he would, he couldn't find any sugar and he couldn't find any syrup. They had been taken away. Only the smell had been left.

In his disappointment Buster lost his temper. He knocked everything down that he could knock down. He upset everything that he could upset. He made just one great mess of everything. By the time he got through doing this he felt better. He left the little house and started out to again look for a place to go to sleep. He didn't know where he was going. He was just wandering and would go to bed at the first good place he saw.

JUST A LITTLE SNOOZE

Life and happiness to keep,
Everybody has to sleep.
              —Old Mother Nature.

BUSTER BEAR had been in mischief. He had nearly wrecked the sugarhouse of Farmer Brown. Probably he didn't think he was in mischief. You see, Buster Bear is in the habit of tearing things to pieces in order to get what he wants. He tears open old stumps and old logs to get at Mice that might be hiding in them. He tears open hollow trees to get at honey, of which he is very fond. You see, the honeybees often make their homes in hollow trees and store away a great deal of honey there. If there is any one thing Buster delights in more than any other, it is a feast of honey.

So it was that when Buster, sniffing around

the cracks of the little sugarhouse, got the smell of sugar and syrup which still clung inside the little house, he saw no wrong in tearing that little house to pieces to get in there. When he got in, there was no sugar, no syrup, only the smell of them, and in his disappointment he lost his temper. Then he smashed those things that could be smashed.

When he left the little sugarhouse he was mostly over his fit of bad temper. He left the grove of maple trees and made his way back farther into the Green Forest. He wasn't going anywhere in particular. He seldom is going anywhere in particular. He is too happy-go-lucky for that. He just wanders about.

Presently Buster began to feel sleepy. He had wandered well back in the Green Forest toward the foot of the Great Mountain. He had been shuffling along the Crooked Little Path because it was easier walking there. The Crooked Little Path leads from the edge of the Green Forest to the foot of the Great Mountain and part way up it. Buster began to feel sleepy. Buster is one of those people who does things when he feels like doing them. If he feels sleepy he lies down and takes a nap, and it doesn't make the least bit of difference what time of the day or night it is. So, now, as he shuffled along, turning his head from side to side, he was looking for a comfortable place to lie down.

After a while Buster came to a sharp turn in the Crooked Little Path. He left it there and wandered off to one side until after a while he came to where a ledge of rock came out from the hillside far enough to make a roof over anyone who might lie down under it. It was more or less surrounded by trees and brush. It was a secluded place. A secluded place, you know, is one which is seldom visited when one is likely not to be disturbed. Buster had napped more than once in that very place. Just seeing it made him still more sleepy. He reached out with first one big paw and then the other and raked in some leaves from the ground. He raked these under that shelf of rock to make a bed. It wouldn't have been much of a bed for you or me, but it suited Buster. And after all, he was the one to be suited.

Buster lay down and yawned. It was a long yawn. "I'll just take a little snooze," said he, and in a few minutes he was fast asleep.

WHAT THE MERRY LITTLE BREEZES DID

Merry Little Breezes play,
But they also work each day.
                    —Old Mother West Wind.

THE MERRY Little Breezes are the children of Old Mother West Wind and they are busy little folk. It is true that they spend a lot of time dancing among the flowers, tripping over the grass so that it makes little waves like the ripples on water. But they do a lot of work too. They blow great ships across the sea. They spin windmills that pump water. They dry Mother's clothes on the clothesline. They dance in at windows and cool those who are sick and cannot get outside.

The Merry Little Breezes had started out very early this morning. It was a dark gloomy morning. It was cold. Yes, sir, it was cold, but not too cold. Presently little snowflakes came sifting down from the dark clouds overhead. The Merry Little Breezes began blowing them about. It was fun. The faster the lovely little snowflakes drifted down the more fun it was to blow them. It was fun to make little drifts of them and see who could build the biggest drift.

Over in the Green Forest the Merry Little Breezes, dancing around among the trees, made a discovery. They found Buster Bear asleep. He was lying on a bed of dead leaves under a shelf of rock at the foot of a hillside. Some of them danced underneath and ruffled up his fur, but he didn't know it. Some of them blew through his whiskers, but he didn't know that either. Some of them even blew in his ears, but they couldn't even make him twitch once. Buster was really sound asleep. He had lain down there for just a little snooze, but that little snooze had turned into a sound sleep. He didn't know a thing about anything that was going on, so of course he didn't know that snow had begun to fall. Perhaps had he known it, he wouldn't have been too happy. You see, snow covers everything, including most of the things Buster most likes to eat.

Two or three Merry Little Breezes dancing along that way blew some little snowflakes in beneath that shelf of rock. They fell on Buster's black coat and looked whiter than ever. Other Little Breezes joined them and blew in more.

"I'll tell you what—let's cover him up. Let's pretend we're putting him to bed," cried a Merry Little Breeze.

"Oh, let's!" cried the other Little Breezes, gathered around.

So they all blew and blew and blew as they danced back and forth. And every time they blew, a lot of little snowflakes fell on Buster's black coat, until at last it looked as if he were wearing a white coat instead of a black coat. And still the Merry Little Breezes danced and blew. This was fun. Little by little, Buster Bear was covered. After a while there was nothing of him to be seen.

"We'll give him a nice, white, thick blanket to keep him warm," cried the Merry Little Breezes. So they kept on dancing and blowing until Buster was buried deep. And all the time he knew nothing about it.

PUTTING BUSTER
BEAR TO BED

A goodly deed for others done
Is proof of friendship truly won.
                    —Old Mother West Wind.

THE MERRY Little Breezes were having fun. Yes, sir, they were having fun. They were putting Buster Bear to bed. Anyway, that is the way they felt about it. They were covering him up with a nice warm blanket. It was a white blanket—a blanket of snow.

You didn't know that snow could keep anybody warm? It can and it does. Way on top of the world, where there is snow and ice most of the year, the people who live there build houses of blocks of snow. A house built of snow is called an igloo. Inside an igloo folks keep warm and comfortable.

Buster Bear was asleep under a ledge of rock at the foot of a hill deep in the Green Forest. The little snowflakes came sifting down through the bare branches of the trees. The Merry Little Breezes whirled them about and blew them under the shelf under Buster. They blew and they blew and they blew. They covered Buster's black coat until he looked as if he were wearing a white coat. They blew and they blew the little snowflakes.

"More!" cried a Merry Little Breeze, and blew hard.

"More!" cried another Merry Little Breeze, and blew harder.

Then all the Merry Little Breezes together blew a lot of little snowflakes over Buster at one time.

That thick white blanket grew thicker and thicker. It covered Buster so deeply that not even his shape could be seen any longer. It looked just like a heap of snow under that rocky ledge.

It was fun and the Merry Little Breezes were having a good time. When they first found him, Buster was asleep and now and then he snored. Now they couldn't hear him. This was because that blanket was so deep.

"We'll bury him deep, to be sure he will sleep," cried a Little Merry Breeze.

Faster and faster fell the little snowflakes. They whirled and they swirled. The Merry Little Breezes danced and swirled with them. They huffed and they puffed. And with every huff and puff a lot of little snowflakes were whirled in to pile up on Buster Bear.

At long last the Merry Little Breezes grew tired. They stopped dancing. They stopped huffing and puffing. They stopped blowing. Presently Old Mother West Wind carried them off in her bag which looks like a cloud.

Then the little snowflakes fell straight down. It was very still there in the Green Forest. Everything was white, and none of all the Green Forest folk knew where Buster Bear had gone to bed. It was a secret that only the Merry Little Breezes knew. And they never would tell.

A WARM COLD BLANKET

Though hard it be to think it so,
There can be comfort in the snow.
                              —Old Mother Nature.

IT WAS midwinter. It was cold. It was very
cold. Ice covered the pond of Paddy the
Beaver deep in the Green Forest. It covered
the Smiling Pool on the Green Meadows. It
covered much of Laughing Brook. It even
covered a great deal of the Big River.

Jack Frost was around night and day. Old
Man Winter really had settled down to stay.
The Green Forest and the Green Meadows
were no longer green, but were white. Beauti-
ful and sparkling white were they. This was
because snow covered everything deep.

Now snow is cold. Yet snow can keep folks warm. Doesn't that seem funny? But it is true. You just ask Buster Bear the next time you meet him. That is, if you ever do meet him. You won't if he sees you first and probably he will. Buster is very bashful at times.

Buster had gone to bed under a shelf of rock deep in the Green Forest. He had lain down just for a little snooze. He was still snoozing. Soon after he went to sleep the snowflakes came sifting down through the trees. Mother West Wind's children, the Merry Little Breezes, had great fun blowing the dancing, whirling little snowflakes in under the shelf until Buster was completely covered. Then they kept on blowing so as to make that white blanket thick. You know, the thicker a blanket is the warmer it is. And all the time Buster Bear knew nothing about it. He never once opened his eyes. That cold blanket really was keeping him warm and he was very, very comfortable. By and by the snow was so deep over and around Buster that, had you happened along that way, you wouldn't have known a Bear was in the neighborhood.

Now in another part of the Green Forest

was a great pile of fallen trees blown over by
a great wind some time in the past. They had
fallen this way and that way on each other.
This made a great pile, called a windfall by
some folks and a blow-down by others.

Underneath this windfall, Mr. Buster Bear
had made a passage. Right under the middle
of the great pile was an open space on the

ground big enough for Mother Bear, and her two children who were spending the winter with her, to sleep close together. They had been asleep before Buster Bear was and had been abed and asleep some time before Buster lay down for that little snooze. Lying close together, they kept each other warm. They had gone to sleep for the winter, although they didn't know it.

Above them the tangled branches of the old windfall kept away Rough Brother North Wind. That was a big help in making them comfortable. When the snow fell, the Merry Little Breezes tried hard to blow it down between the branches over them to make a white blanket for them. They couldn't make that blanket as fast as the one they did over Buster Bear, but they did make a good start. Then Old Mother West Wind gathered them up and carried them away.

But the little snowflakes continued to fall straight down. They sifted down through the branches of the old windfall and continued to make that white blanket thicker. With every snowstorm after that the same thing happened. So it was that Mother Bear and the cubs also slept warm under a cold blanket.

REDDY FOX JUMPS

Wise the Fox who always knows,
What is told him by his nose.

— Reddy Fox.

REDDY FOX was hunting down in the Green Forest. As a rule, he likes to hunt in open country rather than in the deep woods. Now and then, however, he makes a trip deep in the Green Forest. He was doing this now.

Now if anyone knows how to use eyes and ears and nose, it is Reddy Fox. He was using all three now. Long, long ago he learned that the faintest of sounds may lead to something very good if followed up. On the other hand, it may lead to something very bad if it is not heeded. So those pointed black ears of Reddy's are always wide open and listening.

It is the same way with his eyes. Anything that moves, however little, may have an important meaning. As he trots along, listening and looking, his nose is always at work. Every **Merry Little Breeze** that comes along is tested for any scent, good or bad, that it may be carrying.

As Reddy trotted along, he saw off to one side a snow-covered ledge of rock near the bottom of a little hill. He turned aside to have a look at it. There might be someone he wanted to catch under that little ledge. When he got close to it he could see under it everywhere. There was no one there. At least, there was no one in sight. He stood perfectly still, listening. There wasn't a sound. There was no listening little leaves, for the trees were bare. He lifted his black little nose. He sniffed and sniffed. At first he could smell nothing. He was just going to move on when a mischievous Merry Little Breeze tickled that little black nose and made Reddy Fox jump as if he had suddenly stepped on something hot. He jumped and ran off to one side a few steps, then turned and stared hard under that little ledge. He saw nothing but snow. He heard nothing. He lifted his nose high and sniffed. There was no startling smell now.

Step by step, step by step, with a pause between each step, Reddy moved toward that overhanging shelf of rock. Beneath it he could still see nothing but snow, just a smooth white blanket of snow. His ears still told him nothing. Until he went back to the place where he had jumped, his nose told him nothing. Then once more a Merry Little Breeze tickled his nose and Reddy jumped, just as he had done before.

"Bear!" exclaimed Reddy. "I smell Bear."

Reddy looked all around suspiciously, but there was no sign of Bear. He circled to both ends of that little ledge, all the time looking and listening. He no longer smelled Bear. However, back at the place where he had smelled it before, he smelled it again.

"As sure as my coat is red, I smell Buster Bear," muttered Reddy. Then Reddy very slowly followed up that Merry Little Breeze to see where that scent was coming from. Then what do you think it led him to? A very small hole in the snow. That was what that scent was coming out of.

COUSIN GRAY IS CURIOUS

There's often gain in finding out,
Just what your neighbors are about.
—Reddy Fox.

GRAY FOX is cousin of Reddy Fox, but in many ways he is quite different from Reddy. For one thing, he loves the Green Forest and doesn't care much for the open country. On the other hand, Reddy Fox doesn't care so much for the Green Forest. They are not friendly, these two. That is too bad. It is always too bad when relatives do not get along together.

Cousin Gray does something that Reddy doesn't do. Cousin Gray climbs trees. He often climbs high in a tree. Once in a while Reddy may get up in some low branches, but that is all. Cousin Gray, on the other hand, spends a lot of time up in trees. He is sometimes called Tree Fox instead of Gray Fox.

It happened that Cousin Gray was up in a tree quite deep in the Green Forest when he saw Cousin Reddy coming his way. He didn't like it. He felt that Reddy was what is called intruding. He was hunting where he had no business to be hunting. Of course this wasn't true, because Reddy had a right to hunt where he pleased, just as did Cousin Gray himself. Reddy felt that the Green Forest belonged to him, so he watched Cousin Reddy suspiciously.

Not far from the tree, high up in which Cousin Gray had made himself comfortable in a big crotch, was a snow-covered ledge of rock near the bottom of a little hill. Years before, a great big wind had blown over lots of trees in such a way that they had fallen on each other, making a great pile. This had gradually settled until it was a tangled heap of brush. At the present time it was covered

with snow, as was the ground all around. The snow-covered ledge had made a great white heap. The snow had blown in under it, making a deep white blanket. Reddy was sniffing around the edge of it. He even ventured a little way up on it. Cousin Gray watched every move that Reddy made. Reddy was sniffing here, sniffing there, hoping perhaps to sniff out a mouse.

Suddenly Reddy jumped. He jumped back as if startled. In fact, he ran back a few steps.

Then he turned and stared at that smooth white blanket of snow under the ledge. He looked startled. Presently he began to move back very slowly. Between each step he paused and sniffed. At the same time he kept looking around suspiciously.

It was clear that something had upset him. Cousin Reddy certainly was acting in a funny way. He was back now to where he had jumped. He stretched his head out with his nose down to the snow. Once more he jumped back, as if startled. Then he turned and trotted away, now and then looking back.

Cousin Gray became more and more curious. "Now, what in the world is the matter with Reddy Fox?" thought he. "He acts as if he is startled, perhaps a little afraid. But there's nothing under that old ledge to be afraid of. I have visited it more times than I can remember."

For some time Cousin Gray remained where he was, but all the time he was growing more and more curious. Finally he decided he would have a look for himself. He climbed down the tree. At the foot of it he hesitated. Then he began to move slowly toward the old ledge.

COUSIN GRAY JUMPS, TOO

Of course, it isn't nice to spy,
Even though it may be fun to try.
                    —Old Mother Nature.

OLD MOTHER NATURE is very right about that. As a rule, spying isn't a nice thing to do. No one likes to have other folks watching them and that is what spying is. But sometimes it is necessary.

Cousin Gray had been spying on Reddy Fox, but that was no more than Reddy would have done to Cousin Gray—and often does. Each tries to find out what the other is doing.

It happened that Cousin Gray was up in a tree. You know he likes to climb. He watched Reddy make his way over the snow-covered ledge. Reddy went in under that ledge in the hope of finding a mouse. Instead he found something that startled him and made him jump back quickly. He not only jumped back, but he ran back a little way. After a while he ventured in a second time and the same thing happened. Then Reddy trotted away with many backward looks.

"Now what could there be under that ledge to make Cousin Reddy act that way?" The more he wondered about it, the more curious Gray Fox became. He simply had to find out.

In front of the ledge he stopped. He has very good eyes, has Gray Fox, and he used them now. But he could see nothing but snow in under that ledge. He used his nose, his trusty nose, through which he learns so much about what is going on about him. There was no telltale smell. He started to go in under that ledge, stopping between every step just as Cousin Reddy had done. Every time he stopped he sniffed. He was well under that shelf when he caught the first faint smell and it was strangely disturbing. It was too faint for him to be sure what it was. He went forward a few more steps and then just a little way ahead of him he saw a small hole in the snow. He stretched out his nose toward this and took a long sniff. What do you think happened then? Why, Cousin Gray did exactly what Cousin Reddy had done. He jumped back as if he had been stung on the end of his nose. In fact, he almost lost his balance, he jumped back so quickly. Then, like Cousin Reddy, he ran back a little way and turned to stare back under that ledge.

Somehow Reddy Fox was having difficulty in believing what his nose told him. Yes, sir, he was so. Now if there is anything a Fox can trust, it is his nose. His eyes may fool him sometimes. His ears may fool him sometimes. But his nose never does. Yet it seemed to Gray Fox now that his nose must be fooling him. He stared and stared back underneath the ledge. Then, as Reddy had done, he very, very slowly walked. He didn't go quite as near that little hole this time and he stretched a little farther for another sniff. His nose hadn't fooled him. Once more he jumped back and this time he trotted away.

"Bear!" he muttered. "Buster Bear! I don't know how it can be, but it is."

So it was that the two cousins, Reddy Fox and Gray Fox, found out the secret of where Buster Bear was spending the winter.

THE SHREWD BLACK WATCHER

A little knowledge, if you please,
Does very little more than tease.
                    —Croaker the Raven.

CROAKER the Raven is the big black cousin of Blacky the Crow. But for size, they look very much alike. Croaker is much bigger. He lives deeper in the Green Forest, or farther up on the Great Mountain. A strong, tough old Bird is Croaker the Raven. He is so strong and tough that somehow he manages to live through the hardest winter in spite of snow and ice and bitter storms. A plucky Bird is old Croaker.

Now, to live through a northern winter, a Bird as big as Croaker the Raven must be more than tough. He must be smart. He must be very smart and Croaker is smart. He is one of the smartest of all the folk in the Green

Forest. If he were not, he wouldn't be able to find enough food to live.

There is little that goes on in the Green Forest of which Croaker does not know. He makes it his business to know everything that is going on. He knew that Buster Bear had not gone to bed for the winter as early as usual. He knew when Mrs. Bear and the Cubs went to bed, and just where. At that time Buster Bear was a long way off. He had the wandering foot at that time. And when he has the wandering foot, he travels great distances just for fun. So for a while Croaker didn't know where Buster was or anything about him. He knew when Buster returned and he knew all about how Buster Bear had broken into Farmer Brown's sugarhouse. But somehow he didn't know when Buster went to bed—perhaps because it was at night and Croaker is not like Hooty the Owl, a Night Bird. Anyway, he didn't know what had become of Buster Bear. He guessed that he had gone to sleep for the winter, but where, he had no idea.

Then one day he saw Reddy Fox hunting deep in the Green Forest. It was unusual for Reddy to come so far into the Green Forest

and from a distance Croaker watched. He long ago learned it pays to watch another hunter.

So it was that Croaker the Raven, watching from a distant treetop, saw Reddy Fox go under a snow-covered ledge and suddenly jump out as if startled. He saw him do it all over again and this time trot away. Croaker was just about to fly over to that ledge when he saw Gray Fox do the same thing Reddy had done. He waited only until Gray Fox was out of sight, then flew straight over to that ledge. He perched on the edge of it and stretched down to look under. Those sharp eyes of his saw nothing unusual except a hole in the snow. It was a small hole and around the edge of it, it was icy. At the sight of that little hole in the snow, Croaker knew where Buster Bear was. You see, he knew Buster Bear's habits so well. He knew that that hole was made by Buster Bear's breath melting the snow. He had seen just such a little breathing hole in the snow before.

"So *that's* where the big rascal is," muttered Croaker, and flew away to look for something to eat. Buster being asleep for the winter meant one less hunter for food.

BLACKY IS EXCITED

Absence brings a point of view,
Making home seem wholly new.
—Mrs. Blacky.

IT IS what was called a spring day. Instead of Rough Brother North Wind blowing as hard as he had blown all winter, Gentle Sister South Wind was blowing. The snow was melting. Laughing Brook had really begun to laugh. The Smiling Pool was still covered with ice, but Jerry Muskrat knew that he wouldn't have to swim under ice much longer.

As usual, Blacky the Crow had awakened very early in the morning. He had awakened just as the Black Shadows had begun to leave the Green Forest to go back behind the Purple Hills. For a while Blacky sat right where he had spent the night, up in a spruce tree, hidden under the branches. He was waiting for the last of the Black Shadows to leave. Twice in the night he had been awakened by

Hooty the Owl. If there is anyone of whom Blacky is afraid, more than any other, it is Hooty the Great Horned Owl. With the Black Shadows gone, Hooty would not be likely to be hunting.

Suddenly Blacky lifted his head a little higher. Could it be he heard what he thought he had? He leaned forward, listening. There it was again! Caw! Caw! Caw! It was faint. He could just barely hear it because it was coming from a long distance away. But he knew that voice. He spread his black wings and flew to the tallest tree on the edge of the Green Forest. You should have heard him then. "Caw! Caw! Caw!" he cried at the top of his voice.

Now Blacky's voice is harsh, but somehow there was in it a new note. That is, a note that hadn't been there all winter. It was a note of eagerness and joy, almost a note of sweetness. It was answered at once. And this time that familiar voice was joined by others. That distant cawing was exciting cawing. Blacky knew exactly what it meant. That first voice he had heard was the voice of Mrs. Blacky. And the other voices he was hearing now were the voices of the flock. They had been gone all winter and now they were coming back.

Blacky flew to meet them. Presently his keen eyes saw them with one in the lead. It was Mrs. Blacky. She was flying faster than the others. She was in a hurry to get home. Blacky was excited, but he was hardly more excited than Mrs. Blacky. Blacky had spent the winter alone in the Green Forest because Mrs. Blacky had gone south with the flock when the cold weather came. It was the first time she had ever done this.

"Caw! Caw! Caw! Caw!" cried Blacky.

"Caw! Caw! Caw! Caw!" replied Mrs. Blacky, and tried to fly faster.

Blacky flew to meet her. There was a field bare of snow. They flew down on that and a moment or two later were joined by the rest of the flock. Such an excited cawing as there was then as they gathered around Blacky! You know, for several years Blacky had been the leader of the flock.

Presently Blacky gave a sharp call. Then he took to his wings and so did all the other Crows. With Mrs. Blacky close behind him, just in front of the flock, Blacky led the way back to the Green Forest.

THE DISCOVERY

The unexpected tests the wit,
In finding ways of meeting it.
                    —Blacky the Crow.

MRS. BLACKY had been away all winter. She had gone with the flock a little way south. Blacky had remained behind. Now the flock was back and Mrs. Blacky was glad to be back. She had to visit all the familiar places right away. Then she began to think about nesting. She began to wonder where they would build this year.

"Aren't you in something of a hurry?" asked Blacky.

"No!" retorted Mrs. Blacky. "The sooner we have a family the better."

"It isn't warm weather yet," said Blacky.

"Who cares?" retorted Mrs. Blacky. "The earlier we get family cares out of the way, the sooner we'll be free to do as we please. Have you thought about where we will build this year?"

"No," replied Blacky. "I haven't thought about anything at all. Why should I? You've been away all winter."

"Well, I'm not away now," retorted Mrs. Blacky. "That was a good place where we nested last year. Perhaps we can find another tree over there in that neighborhood that will be as good as the one we used last year."

Blacky nodded his black head. "My dear, I don't believe we could do better," said he. "I haven't been over there all winter, because there was nothing to take me over there. Let's go over there now and look things over."

So together they flew over to a certain lonesome part of the Green Forest where tall pine trees grew and where there were few visitors at any time. One pine tree was extra tall. Mrs. Blacky led the way and headed straight for it. It was in that tree that they had built their stout nest the year before. She wanted to have a look at that old nest again.

She was in such a hurry that she got some distance ahead of Blacky. She had almost reached that tree when she almost turned a somersault in the air in her haste to come back. She was a scared Crow. There was no doubt about that. Blacky saw her coming and waited for her in the nearest tree. He didn't have to wait but a minute.

"My dear," said he, "you look frightened."

"I am and I'm not," replied Mrs. Blacky. "I am when I think how near I came to landing at that nest before I saw who was in it. And I'm not frightened now, because I got safely away."

Blacky looked curious. He was curious. "Did you say someone is in that nest?" he asked.

"Mrs. Hooty the Owl," almost whispered Mrs. Blacky. She would have whispered if she could, but she couldn't. No Bird can whisper.

"Let's get out of here," said Blacky. "Hooty must be around somewhere. I don't like him."

"I don't like either one of them," replied Mrs. Blacky, and led the way back the way they had come.

THE DISAGREEMENT

Most fortunate and smart is he,
Who knows how far to disagree.
                              —Blacky the Crow.

OVER in the Green Forest a noisy argument was going on. It wasn't exactly a quarrel, just an argument. Even so, it wasn't too pleasant to hear, and arguments often lead to too many quarrels. Blacky the Crow and Mrs. Blacky didn't agree. It was all on account of the new nest they must build. They had planned to build it over in the same lonesome part of the Green Forest where they had successfully raised a family the year before. They went over there to have a look at the old nest and made a discovery. It was a startling discovery. That nest was already occupied. Mrs. Hooty the Great Horned Owl had set up housekeeping there—and Hooty and Mrs. Hooty are two folks Blacky and Mrs. Blacky have the greatest respect for. In fact, they are afraid of those two Owls, especially at night.

"Of course," said Mrs. Blacky, "we've got to look for another place to build this year."

"I'm not sure about that," declared Blacky.

"What do you mean?" cried Mrs. Blacky. "You're not dreaming of our building a nest in that neighborhood, are you?"

"It could be the safest place in all the Green Forest," retorted Blacky.

"With those two robbers raising a family over there," cawed Mrs. Blacky, "that is about the most dangerous neighborhood in all the Green Forest!"

"It could be the safest, just as I said before," retorted Blacky. "Those Owls never would look for us in that neighborhood, nor would anybody else. Everybody keeps away from there. We could build in a tree out of sight from where they are, and you know they are not looking around much in daytime. If we never made any noise over there, they might not know we were anywhere near."

"Just the same, I don't like it—and we're not going to build over there," retorted Mrs. Blacky.

"Is there a better place?" asked Blacky.

"I don't know, but if there is, I'll find one," cawed Mrs. Blacky.

"You won't find a place any safer and probably not as safe," declared Blacky. And he said it as if he really meant it. He did. You see, he had almost convinced himself.

So they argued back and forth, not only that day, but for the next two or three days, while they went looking here and there for a place to build. Blacky still insisted he was right. Mrs. Blacky was sure that she was right. And it began to look as if they would never agree.

But Blacky the Crow is one of the smartest people in all the Green Forest. He knew just how far to go in disagreeing with Mrs. Blacky. And then he wisely gave up. "All right, my dear," said he. "You choose the place and I won't say a word."

So it was that Mrs. Blacky chose a certain tree in a part of the Green Forest that was not nearly as lonesome and free of neighbors as was that place where the old nest was and where Hooty and Mrs. Hooty were already nesting. Blacky didn't like it, but he said nothing and did his part in helping to hunt for material to build the new nest.

BLACKY DROPS A STICK

A hint is all some people need,
Straight to the hidden facts to lead.
                    —Old Mother Nature.

BLACKY the Crow and Mrs. Blacky had begun nest building. Mrs. Blacky had chosen a spruce tree with thick-growing branches and had started the nest high up in it. Blacky did not approve of that place. He didn't think it was a lonesome enough place. He was very much afraid that their nest would be discovered by someone who might be able to steal the eggs, or perhaps the babies, if they did not get the eggs.

However, Blacky said nothing and did his part. Blacky and Mrs. Blacky are good workers when they have work to do. Blacky does his part. They know that a good nest must be a stout nest and whenever they build a nest it is a good nest. They use sticks for the foundation. Mrs. Blacky is very fussy about placing those sticks. She knows how to put them together so that none will slip out of place. Blacky left that part of the work to her. He spent his time hunting for the right sticks. She was fussy about the sticks. Now and then Blacky would bring one that didn't suit her. She would just toss it aside. Blacky would say nothing, but go look for another one.

Now, all the time that they were going and coming, both Blacky and Mrs. Blacky kept careful watch to see that no one would suspect what they were doing. They were very careful about this.

Not very far from where that nest was being built lived Chatterer the Red Squirrel. Like other members of the Squirrel family and many others, Chatterer has what he thinks of as his private range. That is, he goes so far in each direction and seldom beyond that. The new nest of Blacky and Mrs. Blacky was a little beyond where Chatterer was in the habit of going. It was just outside his private grounds.

One day, as Chatterer sat in his doorway, he looked up as Blacky flew overhead. Blacky was carrying something in his bill. Just then he dropped it accidentally and it fell right near the foot of the tree in which Chatterer was sitting. He ran down the tree to see what Blacky had droppd. It was a stick, rather a small stick. Chatterer looked up to see if Blacky was coming down after that stick. Blacky wasn't. He was nowhere in sight. He had seen Chatterer and had promptly hurried away. He didn't want Chatterer to be too curious as to what he, Blacky, was doing.

Chatterer looked down at the stick. He chuckled. Yes, sir, he chuckled. "I know what that means," thought he. "Blacky and Mrs. Blacky are building a nest. I must find that nest. A new nest means eggs, sooner or later, and I certainly do like eggs."

Thereafter Chatterer kept watch for Blacky and Mrs. Blacky. Now and then he got a glimpse of them flying over the treetops. Always they went in a certain direction. That stick that Blacky had dropped was a hint of what was going on. And a hint was all that Chatterer needed. He was sure that sooner or later he would be able to find that nest.

CHATTERER HOLDS HIS TONGUE

When noisy tongues are strangely still,
Beware lest it betoken ill.

—Old Mother Nature.

BLACKY the Crow and Mrs. Blacky had finished their new nest. It was a good nest. It was well-placed high in a spruce tree. From the ground looking up, no one was likely to notice it. While building it, the two Crows had been undisturbed. They felt sure that no one knew about that nest.

When the nest was nicely lined with dry grass and a few feathers, Mrs. Blacky laid five eggs therein and began sitting.

Blacky is a good mate. He had done his share in bringing material to build the nest. Now he did his share in sitting on the eggs.

When Mrs. Blacky wanted to get something to eat, Blacky would take her place. "Don't hurry back, my dear. Take your time," he would say. And Mrs. Blacky would.

Now, not far away lived Chatterer the Red Squirrel. Both Blacky and Mrs. Blacky knew all about Chatterer and his ways. They knew that Chatterer has a fondness for eggs. They have, too, for that matter—the eggs of other birds.

Every day they would hear Chatterer scolding in the distance. You know, he is a great scolder. It seems as if he is never truly happy unless he is scolding someone. When there is no one around to scold, he scolds just the same, to hear his own voice.

One morning Mrs. Blacky left to get her breakfast and Blacky took her place in the nest. When she came back, Blacky said, "My dear, do you miss anything?"

Mrs. Blacky looked all around. "What should I miss?" she asked.

"A voice," replied Blacky.

Mrs. Blacky stopped looking and began listening. At first she didn't know what Blacky meant. Then, all in a flash, she knew. "It's Chatterer!" she cried. "That noisy tongue of his is still. What do you suppose that means?"

"Mischief," replied Blacky. "When Chatterer holds his tongue, then watch out."

"I hope the rascal keeps away from here," said Mrs. Blacky.

"I haven't seen him around here. Have you?" said Blacky.

Mrs. Blacky shook her head. "No," said she, "I don't believe he knows we've got a nest over here. I never have seen him as far from home as this. I don't think we need to worry about him at all."

"I would feel more sure of it if I could hear that voice of his. It isn't a pleasant voice, but it does tell one where he is," said Blacky.

After a while Chatterer began scolding again. Blacky and Mrs. Blacky looked relieved. He was back home. But the next morning the same thing happened again. Chatterer was strangely still. Without knowing just why, Blacky and Mrs. Blacky felt uneasy. He was in mischief of some kind, they were sure. They were quite right. While they were talking about him, he was watching from a snug hiding place and trying to plan how he could get those eggs.

TEMPTATION IS TOO GREAT

When tempted, you will always find,
It is a test of strength of mind.

—Old Mother Nature.

CHATTERER the Red Squirrel likes eggs. When his feathered neighbors are nesting, Chatterer is always on the watch for a chance to steal the eggs from their nests. That is one reason he is not liked by the feathered folk. He makes a business of looking for nests being built in the Old Orchard and in his part of the Green Forest. Then he watches for a chance to get the eggs without being seen doing it.

This spring Blacky the Crow and Mrs. Blacky had built a nest high in a tall spruce tree not far from where Chatterer made his home. They had been very careful in building that nest to keep it as much a secret as possible. It was just by chance that Chatterer had found what they were doing. Blacky, carrying a stick for the nest, had dropped it. It had fallen almost in front of Chatterer and he looked up just in time to catch a glimpse of Blacky. He guessed right away that a nest was being built somewhere near. After that he watched until he found just where Blacky and Mrs. Blacky were going.

This morning Chatterer was out early, almost as soon as daylight began to appear. He found a hiding place over near the tree in which that nest was. There he hid, hoping that both Blacky and Mrs. Blacky would leave to get a breakfast, when he would have a chance to go up and see what was in that nest. What he had hoped would happen did happen. The two big black feathered neighbors left together. You see, they had not yet begun sitting on those eggs. Hardly were they out of sight when Chatterer was over at the foot of that tall spruce tree. Should he or should he not climb up to that nest? It wouldn't take but a minute. You know, Chatterer can run up and down trees as fast as some people can run on the ground. It was a great temptation. In fact, it was too great a temptation to resist. If he was quick about it, he could get up to that nest and find out if there were eggs in it before either Blacky or Mrs. Blacky returned. He might even have time to eat a couple. He started up the tree. Halfway up, he stopped to look and listen. The higher he got the oftener he stopped for a hasty look around. He could see nothing of those Crows. He got up to the nest. It was a well-built nest. It was rough looking outside, because the outside was mostly sticks. But when he peeped over the edge and looked into it he saw that it was nicely lined with strips of fine bark, dried grass, moss and other things to make it snug and comfortable.

Chatterer paid no attention to this. All he had eyes for were five big eggs. He gloated. Yes, sir, he just sat on the edge of that nest and gloated. What a feast this would be! He forgot to watch. I suspect he forgot he was up in the top of a tall tree. All he could think of was those eggs and how good they were going to taste. He was just reaching for one when a shadow swept over the nest. He looked up. Then he forgot all about eggs. He lost his appetite right then and there. All he could think of was getting away from there as fast as possible.

A JUMP FOR LIFE

Life, too precious to be lost,
Must be saved at any cost.
　　　　　　—Old Mother Nature.

CHATTERER the Red Squirrel was in trouble. He was in real trouble. It was nothing new for him to be in trouble, because he naturally is full of mischief and seemingly always looking for trouble. He had found it this time. Yes, siree, he had found it this time. He was high up in a tall tree where he had no business to be. He was on the edge of the nest of Blacky the Crow.

It was Chatterer's fondness for eggs that had gotten him into trouble this time. Eggs, when he can find them, are his favorite food in the spring. He had discovered that nest and, watching his chance, had climbed up to it while both Blacky and Mrs. Blacky were away. When he had first looked over the edge of that nest, his eyes had almost popped out of his head. He had hoped that there might be two or three eggs. There were five. What a feast! He was just reaching for one when a shadow passed over. He looked up. There was Mrs. Blacky coming swiftly down from high up in the sky. She had seen him and she was diving straight at him. Chatterer forgot all about eggs. He dodged down under the nest, and just as he did so, Blacky appeared. Then began a game of hunt and dodge, only it wasn't really a game. Blacky and Mrs. Blacky were doing the hunting and Chatterer was doing the dodging. He is quick. He needed to be now. Blacky would dash at him and he would dodge around to the other side of the trunk of the tree. Mrs. Blacky would almost dash at him from that side. Chatterer had no chance to run down that tree. He was fairly trapped. There was only one thing to do. He must jump for his life.

Now, that was a tall tree. It was the tallest tree in that part of the Green Forest. It was a long way from where the nest was to the ground. There was no other tree near enough for him to jump to.

Now, Blacky and Mrs. Blacky were surprisingly quick. Chatterer was having hard work dodging them. He knew that it would be just too bad for him should he be struck by one of those stout bills. He gave a hasty look down. The ground was a long, long way off. He dodged around to the other side and looked down. There was a small pile of brush on the ground on that side. Blacky dashed in and just missed Chatterer with that big black bill of his. Chatterer dodged around to the other side and the same thing happened with Mrs. Blacky. Chatterer knew then that he couldn't keep this up. He would have to jump for his life. A moment later he was around on the side where the brush heap was. He ran out on a limb to the tip and jumped. He spread himself as flat as possible. It was done so suddenly and so unexpectedly that it caught Blacky and Mrs. Blacky by surprise. By the time they realized what Chatterer was doing, and dived after him, he was almost to the ground. He landed with a thump that almost, but not quite, knocked the breath out of him. He still had enough left to run for that pile of brush and crawl under it. For the time being he was safe.

CHATTERER WISHES
HE HADN'T

Merely wishing is in vain.
Nothing will it ever gain.
　　　　　—Old Mother Nature.

THE HEART of Chatterer the Red Squirrel was going pitter-pat, pitter-pat. He had just had a dreadful experience. He was safe now, but only a moment before he had been in the greatest possible danger of losing his life, and all because he had yielded to temptation. He had tried to steal the eggs of Blacky the Crow and Mrs. Blacky. He had had to jump from near the top of the tallest tree anywhere around. He had landed with a thump and then, just in time, had dodged under a pile of brush, where he now was.

Outside that pile of brush, Blacky and Mrs. Blacky were keeping watch. Chatterer couldn't see them because they were watching from too high up in the tree for him to see them. In fact, he couldn't look up at all, on account of the brush. Though he couldn't see them, he knew they were there. You see, he had known Blacky and Mrs. Blacky for a long time and he knew their ways.

"I wish I hadn't found that nest," whimpered Chatterer to himself. "Anyway, I wish I hadn't climbed up to it. I wish I had stayed at home and minded my own business. But I do love eggs. And those eggs up there would have made a wonderful breakfast."

For the moment, thinking of those eggs, Chatterer forgot his present troubles. It was very still over there in that neighborhood. Blacky and Mrs. Blacky, if they weren't anywhere around, were keeping very quiet. He knew how patient they could be. And he knew, too, that now that they knew he knew where their nest was, they would constantly keep watch for him.

For a long time Chatterer kept perfectly still under the brush. Then very, very carefully he crept to where he could peep out. Of

course all he could see was what lay on that side of the pile of brush. He couldn't see what might be on the other side or the back. No one was in sight, but that didn't mean that no one was close by. "I wish I knew where those Crows are," thought Chatterer. "I wish

I knew if they are still watching or if they have gone away."

But these wishes were as vain as the other wishes. Chatterer settled himself to try to be patient and watch. After a long, long time, who should appear but Jumper the Hare. Jumper hopped past just a little way from the pile of brush. He didn't see Chatterer. He wasn't in a hurry, but he was going somewhere and he didn't stop. "I guess those Crows have gone," thought Chatterer. "But I can't be sure. They wouldn't bother Jumper, so they may still be sitting, waiting for me. I don't know how I'm ever going to find out whether or not they have gone."

Meanwhile, Mrs. Blacky had gone back to those precious eggs in the nest. But Blacky hadn't. He had merely gone a little farther away and settled himself in a tree from which he could watch and see Chatterer, should he come out from under that pile of brush. He meant to teach the little red-coated scamp a lesson he would never forget. He would teach him not to try to steal eggs. The queer thing about it is, that Blacky himself is a stealer of eggs. He, too, likes eggs for breakfast, as lots of smaller feathered folk know.

WHAT DID IT MEAN?

The unknown, not the known, 'tis clear,
Is always cause of greatest fear.
　　　　　　　　—Old Mother Nature.

CHATTERER, the noisy red-coated scamp of the Green Forest, was a scared and worried little Squirrel. He was under a small pile of brush in the Green Forest, a prisoner of his own fear. He had been in mischief and he was paying for it. Folks who get in mischief usually have to pay for it, but some never seem to learn this. Chatterer is one of these. This time he had tried to steal the eggs of Blacky the Crow and had had to jump for his life from high up in a tall tree. He had been lucky to get under that pile of brush before Blacky or Mrs. Blacky could catch him. Now he had to stay there because he didn't dare come out in the open. He was sure those Crows were watching for him, although he couldn't see them.

"If I only knew where those Crows are, I would know better what to do," thought Chatterer. "It may be they have gone away, but how am I to know? If they haven't gone, they will go if I stay here long enough. But how am I to know what long enough is?"

At long last he ventured to poke his head outside. For a long time he sat there with just his head out, looking and listening. His usually noisy tongue was still. Yes, sir, it was still. Finally he ventured out wholly and sat up. He looked this way. He looked that way. He listened. It was very still there. He was almost ready to venture a little farther out when he heard a sound that sent him scampering back under the brush in a hurry. He was sure it was the harsh voice, though faint, of Blacky the Crow. It wasn't. It was the sound of two limbs rubbing together in the wind, for Old Mother West Wind had begun to blow. It was a long time before Chatterer ventured out again.

"If only I knew where those Crows are," thought Chatterer. "It is not knowing that gives me the most fear. Knowing, I would know what to do. Not knowing, I don't know what to do. It may be that it is perfectly safe for me to run home. But it may be that if I try, I will run straight into danger. I wish I knew what to do."

Chatterer had spent most of the day underneath that pile of brush. Now it was getting late in the afternoon. It wouldn't be long before the first of the Black Shadows came creeping into the Green Forest. He was getting more and more anxious to get home, but he was still uncertain about those Crows. He was sitting just outside the brush, but close to it, when, happening to look up through the treetops, he caught a glimpse of Blacky the Crow. Blacky was flying away in a hurry.

"I wonder what he's flying like that for?" thought Chatterer. "If only Mrs. Blacky was with him, I could go home. I wish I knew where she is."

All of this time, Mrs. Blacky was sitting on the eggs that Chatterer had tried to steal. She had left it to Blacky to watch for Chatterer while she took care of those precious eggs. But, of course, Chatterer didn't know this. So he still remained where he was and wondered why Blacky had left in such a hurry. Should he or should he not try to get home now?

CHATTERER FINDS OUT

Some things we gain were better lost;
We get them at too great a cost.

— Chatterer.

BLACKY the Crow had gone. He had left in a hurry. Anyway, that is how it seemed to Chatterer the Red Squirrel and he wondered about it. Blacky had kept Chatterer a prisoner under a pile of brush for a long time. Now he had disappeared over the tree-tops and he had been flying fast.

"I wonder if he is simply tired of watching for me and is in a hurry to get home," thought the little Squirrel in the red coat. "It looked to me more as if he was afraid of something or someone."

Chatterer was sitting just outside that pile of brush where he could dive back under it in a hurry if he had to. Now he looked this way and that way, wherever he could, but he saw no one of whom Blacky might be afraid. He couldn't see over the pile of brush behind him unless he went a little farther out from it. And he was still uncertain about Mrs. Blacky. He would have felt better had he known that she had gone home long ago to sit on her precious eggs. But he didn't know, so for a while he sat right there, close to that pile of brush. He was just about to venture a little farther out for a better look around when Hooty, biggest of all the Owl folk, lighted on top of a tall stub just a little way off. Chatterer dodged back under the brush in a hurry. Hooty was more to be feared than Blacky the Crow. Much more.

"So that is who Blacky was flying from. No wonder he was in a hurry," thought Chatterer. "I would have left in a hurry if I had been in his place. It must be that Mrs. Blacky has gone too. She wouldn't stay with that fellow around. Now all I have to do is wait until he flies off and then I can go home."

Chatterer had never had such a chance to see the big Owl as he had now. He could see the great curved claws peeping out from the feathers that covered Hooty's toes. He could see the big hooked bill. Just seeing these things sent little shivers all over him. Of all the hunters with wings there is none that looks or is more fierce than Hooty the Great Horned Owl. On the top of that old dead stump he turned his head from side to side as his big yellow eyes looked this way and that. Sometimes it seemed as if he turned his head completely around. Of course he didn't. But he did turn it so far that he could look straight back of him. Then he would turn it back so quickly that it did look as if his head went all the way around.

How long would Hooty stay there? Chatterer wished he knew. He wouldn't dare try to get home as long as Hooty was there. He would hardly dare to poke his nose out. It was getting late. Chatterer doesn't like to be out after dark. How he did wish he had never thought of trying to get those eggs of Blacky and Mrs. Blacky.

Off in the distance he heard the voice of Blacky. Then he heard answering voices from different directions. They sounded excited. Chatterer wondered why. "If I were Blacky, I'd keep awfully still," thought Chatterer, as he looked over at the big Owl.

THE WELCOME GANG

The quick to see a chance and take it
Will very seldom fail to make it.
> —Old Mother Nature.

ON TOP of a tall dead stub of a tree in the Green Forest sat Hooty the Owl. He looked much like a part of that old dead stub. Under a pile of brush just a little way from him was Chatterer the Red Squirrel. He had been kept a prisoner there for a large part of the day, first by Blacky the Crow and Mrs. Blacky, whose eggs he had tried to steal, and now by Hooty. The big Owl didn't know he was keeping Chatterer a prisoner. He didn't even know Chatterer was there. But Chatterer knew that Hooty was there and he didn't dare come out from under that brush.

Blacky the Crow had left in a hurry when Hooty arrived. Blacky was as much afraid of the big fierce Owl as was Chatterer. That is, he was afraid when he was alone. Now Chatterer could hear Blacky calling to his friends, the Black Gang, as they were known in the Green Forest. They were answering from all directions.

The harsh cawing of those voices sounded nearer. Could it be that the gang was coming that way? It could be and was. All of a sudden the air seemed to be full of big flapping wings. And such a racket as those Crows made! They began flying around Hooty the Owl, all screaming at the tops of their voices. Hooty was snapping his head around, first this way and then that, to keep watching those Crows. Chatterer could hear the sound of Hooty's big bill as he opened and shut it with a snap. He has a way of doing that when he is angry.

There is nothing slow about Chatterer's wits. "I never thought that that Black Gang would be welcome in my neighborhood. No, sir, I never did. But they are this time. They are giving me a chance, if I am smart enough to take it," said Chatterer to himself.

He crept out from the brush a little, ready
to dart back in a hurry if it was necessary.
Hooty was much too occupied with those
Crows to be watching anything else. And
those Crows had eyes only for the big Owl.

Keeping close to the pile of brush, Chatterer crept around it until it was between him and the Black Gang. Then he took to his heels—and how he did run! He had seen his chance and was making the most of it. He didn't stop running until he had reached his own home tree. There he did stop to listen. He could still hear the screaming of the Black Gang. Of course he could not hear the sound of Hooty's snapping bill, which had made the little shivers run over him when he was near enough to hear it.

Chatterer wished that he could see just what the Black Gang was doing to that big Owl. He really didn't know just which would win if they should fight. He hated Hooty the Owl, but he had no love for Blacky the Crow and his friends.

Meanwhile, Hooty was having a most uncomfortable time. He wasn't afraid of those Crows, but they did make him most uncomfortable. They even dared to pull out two or three of his feathers. He had lost his temper completely. He was waiting and watching for a chance to get one of his tormentors. They, on their part, were having fun. Anyway, they thought they were.

THE PRICE OF FUN

Dangerous fun just doesn't pay,
Precious lives are lost that way.
                    —Old Mother Nature.

BLACKY the Crow's Black Gang was making a lot of trouble for Hooty the Great Horned Owl. There were old Crows and young Crows in the gang. All were having fun, or thought they were. Some people seem to find fun in making other folks feel miserable. It was so with the members of the gang.

The older Crows were more careful than the younger ones. They were taking few chances. They didn't go too close to Hooty. They knew well what could happen and might happen. But it wasn't so with the younger members of the gang.

One was especially daring. He was a silly young Crow. He was trying to show off. And it is always silly to show off. He was more daring than any of the others and he was taking more risks.

"If you are not careful, you'll be sorry!" Blacky warned the young show-off.

"I'm not afraid. I can take care of myself," retorted the young Crow pertly, and almost brushed Hooty's face with one of his wings.

"You'll do that once too often," warned another old Crow.

The young Crow took no heed. Twice he had darted in from behind and pulled a feather from the back of Hooty's coat.

"There's nothing to be afraid of," boasted the young Crow. "Watch me get another feather."

The other times when he had pulled feathers it had been while Hooty was giving all his attention to other Crows. This time when the young Crow darted in to pull a feather there was a difference. Hooty was watching him and not the other Crows. Hooty had been sure that sooner or later the foolish young Crow would make the mistake of being too bold. He made that mistake right now. He had been having what he thought was fun, but he had to pay too great a price for it. Just what happened, happened so quickly that no one saw just how it did happen. Suddenly there were two Owls instead of one. Mrs. Hooty had dashed in and caught that foolish young Crow. He didn't have a chance in the world. He paid with his life for what he had called fun. It happens almost every day all over the Great World.

Such an outcry as there was then! Every Crow went flying for his life. They scattered, flying in all directions. There would be no more tormenting of Hooty that day. Together the two big Owls flew back to that lonesome corner of the Green Forest where their nest was.

"I guess," said Mrs. Hooty, "that that will teach those Crows a lesson."

"I'm sure it will," replied Hooty. "There wasn't much I could do, but you got them by surprise. I was hoping you would hear the racket and come, my dear."

"I was afraid that what happened would happen," said Blacky to Mrs. Blacky when they were together a little later. "Young folks often do such silly things."

"You were young yourself once," said Mrs. Blacky.

Blacky said nothing more.